P9-CFU-131
the VANISHING COIN
the Magic Shop

Kate Egan

with **Magician Mike Lane**

illustrated by **Eric Wight**

Imprints of Macmillan Publishing Group, LLC
175 Fifth Avenue, New York, NY 10010
mackids.com

Printed in the United States of America by LSC Communications,
Harrisonburg, Virginia

Library of Congress Cataloging-in-Publication Data is available.

Originally published in the United States by Feiwel and Friends
First Square Fish edition, 2014
Book designed by Véronique Lefèvre Sweet
Square fish logo designed by Filomena Tuosto

ISBN 978-1-250-02914-0 (Feiwel and Friends hardcover)
10 9 8 7 6

ISBN 978-1-250-04043-5 (Square Fish paperback)
10

For Jean, who waved her magic wand.

—K. E.

To Evelyn, whose last words to me were
"You'll show them all." She believed.

—M. L.

the VANISHING COIN

the Magic Shop

NCIPAL

Chapter 1

IN TROUBLE AGAIN

Nine-year-old Mike Weiss slumped in a hard chair outside the principal's office. Fourth grade was supposed to be a fresh start, but he was right back where he always was. Every year since kindergarten, at least once a week. In trouble.

He wasn't a bad kid. He wasn't mean. He didn't hurt anyone. He just couldn't sit still. Sometimes he did things without meaning to.

When he had gotten up and walked around during the math test, he really wasn't looking at anybody's paper. He just had to move! But that was against the rules, and he had ignored his teacher's warning, so here he was.

Over the summer, he'd been working on ways to cope. "Strategies," his parents called them. Sometimes they worked, and sometimes they didn't. It looked like the strategies weren't going to change things at school, though. It just wasn't fair.

The principal was on the phone, behind a closed door. Any minute that door would fly open and the same routine would start all over again. Calling his parents. Talking about consequences. Making a plan.

Mike kicked the bottom rung of his chair until Mrs. Warren, the school secretary, glanced up. Then he stared at the floor. There was a bare spot in the rug beneath his feet. Was he the one wearing it thin?

Mrs. Warren had a jar of candy on her desk. Mike wasn't supposed to eat sugar, but one little piece couldn't hurt, right? He got up and helped himself to a chocolate kiss. It made him feel a little better, and Mrs. Warren never minded. She usually left the discipline to the principal.

"Who's your teacher this year, Mike?" she asked kindly.

"Mrs. Canfield," he answered. "She seems nice." He really meant it, too. Until a few minutes ago, he'd thought that maybe Mrs. Canfield would understand him.

"You're going to love her!" said Mrs. Warren. She started putting flyers in the teachers' mailboxes. "She just needs to get to know you," she added. Mrs. Warren knew all about Mike's problems. She had a son just like him, she said. Right down to the brown eyes and the messy hair.

Some first graders walked in with an attendance sheet, staring at him like he was some kind of criminal. That was bad enough. Then Mike heard a class coming down the hall. One of the other fourth-grade teachers was at the front of the line, reminding the kids to be quiet as they made their way to the art room. Before they passed, Mike ducked behind a file cabinet in the office. But it was too late.

"Mike!" a girl called, her ponytail bouncing.

"Hey, Nora," Mike muttered. Her family had recently moved next door to his, and she was just his age. Just his luck.

"Going home sick?" Nora asked. She would never be in the office for any other reason. Nora was gifted, his mom had told him. She needed special classes and extra-challenging

homework. She could handle sitting quietly at a desk.

Mike didn't think Nora seemed any different from most kids. She was friendly, and she liked to play four-square. He might have liked her if he didn't know she was good at everything she tried. They definitely didn't have that in common.

"Not exactly sick . . ." he said. It was hard to explain. Luckily Nora's teacher was moving her along.

"See you after school!" she said, waving good-bye.

Mike looked around to make sure nobody had heard that. It was still a new arrangement, and he hoped it wouldn't last. He and Nora weren't really friends, but their parents were. They'd hit it off from the day Nora's family moved in. It only took a couple of backyard barbecues before their mothers had cooked up a plan to help each other out after school.

Both sets of parents had flexible schedules, but they couldn't always pick their kids up at three o'clock. So now Nora came to Mike's house when her parents were busy, and Mike went to Nora's when his were. He was going there today, actually. Another fun afternoon of raw vegetables and no screen time at Nora's.

The principal's door was still closed. Mrs. Warren was making a fresh pot of coffee. Mike wondered what his mom had told Nora's. If Nora was gifted, what was he? What was the opposite?

The idea made him so mad that he didn't notice the shadow in the office doorway. It still wasn't the principal. It was much worse. Jackson Jacobs, Mike's enemy since birth, was shaking his head. "Not again!" Jackson said. "It's only the first week of school, man. You're in trouble already?"

Last year Jackson had been in Mike's class. Mike hadn't seen him all summer, even though they lived in the same neighborhood. It looked like Jackson had grown about a foot at camp.

He always knew how to get under Mike's skin. "Hey, where were you at soccer practice?" Jackson asked. For once, he waited to hear what Mike had to say.

Mike gulped. "I'm not playing this year," he said.

"Not playing?" said Jackson, amazed. "But you always play. Charlie and Zack are playing. I saw them on the field."

Mike's best friends, Charlie and Zack, had already given him a hard time. They were on the same team this year, with matching orange jerseys, numbers 12 and 13. "I need to focus on my schoolwork," Mike said. "Soccer is a big commitment."

"Is that what your parents said?" asked Jackson. "So it has nothing to do with the way you never got a goal, right?" He punched Mike playfully on the arm. "What's wrong with you, big guy? Skipping soccer is never going to help your schoolwork. It'll take a lot more than that!"

Jackson headed toward the boys' bathroom, laughing like it was the funniest thing he'd ever heard.

And of course that's when the principal's phone call finally ended. Mike saw the doorknob turning and Ms. Scott's sensible shoes marching toward him. He sat up straight and tried to smile.

"Welcome back," she said, waving him into her office like he was an old friend. He sat down in his usual place in front of her desk, and she sat down in her huge chair. He felt like he was back in preschool. Ms. Scott sighed deeply.

"I don't know what to say, Mike," she began. "It's too early in the year for this. Your mom said you made good progress over the summer. What happened?"

"I don't know," Mike said honestly. "I was taking a test and I needed to get up. I wasn't cheating or anything. I was just . . . moving."

"We need to find a way for you to succeed in school," Ms. Scott explained, not for the first time. "You can't keep roaming around during tests, or missing assignments, or fooling around in class. You need to find a way to focus."

What could Mike say? "I know . . ." he trailed off.

"I'll need to call your parents," Ms. Scott said. "Mrs. Canfield and I will meet with them as soon as we can find a date."

Mike's parents had already tried a million ways to keep him "on task," as they said. They'd set alarms to go off whenever he had to start a new activity. They made him eat healthy food and get more sleep. Nothing did the trick. "They're already trying," Mike said softly.

"I know they are," said Ms. Scott. "But I know you can do better."

When he finally left the office, Mike tried to look on the bright side. She hadn't said "I'm disappointed in you." She hadn't said "You need to concentrate," like he could just flip a switch. She was trying to say she believed in him. That he could really do it somehow.

But mostly Mike heard Jackson's words ringing in his ears. "What's wrong with you?" He couldn't play soccer, it was true. He couldn't sit still. Or read a long book. Or remember his math facts. Or get through a week of school without ending up in the office. What was wrong with him? Mike wondered.

The answer was pretty simple: everything.

Chapter 2
THE WHITE RABBIT

When the bell rang, Mike left school alone. Usually he walked home with Charlie and Zack, but now they had soccer practice twice a week. It was strange to walk through their neighborhood by himself. He knew the people inside every house, but he was totally alone.

Mike wondered what his friends were doing without him. Running loops around the field? Dribbling the ball around orange cones?

He wondered if Jackson's team was practicing, too. Mike really didn't want to run into him right now. He just wanted this day to end.

At Nora's back door, he took his shoes off, left them on the porch, and let himself in. Her family had a lot of rules. No shoes in the house. No snacks with artificial ingredients. No fun till the homework was done.

But today Mrs. Finn, Nora's mom, was standing by the door with her car keys. "There's been a change in plans, Mike," she said. "I need to get to the dentist, and it turns out he can fit me in right now. You and Nora will come along, too. Leave your backpack right here and get in the car, okay?"

Mike shrugged. "Sounds good," he said. He was glad he wouldn't be stuck at Nora's.

Nora walked into the kitchen, holding her mom's phone. "We can play games while we're there!" she told Mike. "My mom said it was okay."

Usually, video games weren't allowed. So Mike felt happy for about a second. Then he saw the game Nora had chosen: Scrabble. Of course, he thought. Just like her. Shooting games were against the rules . . . and those were the only kind he liked.

The backseat of the van was quiet while Nora tried to make a word. Mike stared out the window as they passed the college where his parents worked. They were teaching right now. Had Ms. Scott called them yet? he wondered.

Mrs. Finn took a right turn, away from downtown. She drove past the ice-cream stand that had just closed and the waterfront restaurant that had been crowded only last month with tourists eating lobster.

The cold season was beginning to set in. By November, people would be hibernating, only coming out to buy more groceries. Winter in Maine was dark and mysterious, Mike's favorite part of the year.

Nora handed him the phone. She'd used all seven of her letters to make the word "erasers." "Fifty points for using them all up," she said. "Your turn."

Mike's letters were all vowels. What words had only vowels? Maybe Nora knew, but he sure didn't. He was tired of looking stupid.

A1 A1 E1 O1 U1 A1 E1

He shifted restlessly in his seat. Mike's mind was so full of worries that he couldn't find a comfortable thought. The principal. His parents. Jackson. Nora. Scrabble. Each one made him squirm.

When they arrived, there were a few other people in the dentist's waiting room, and the woman behind the desk had too much to do. "Yes, Mrs. Finn," she said. "I know I said now. But there were two patients in line before you . . ."

Those patients glared at Mike as he drummed on the arm of his chair. Nora nudged him. "What about your word?" she asked. She sounded just like a teacher.

"I'm skipping my turn," he said, handing her the phone. "Giving up all my letters and taking more."

"You know you have to subtract points from your score?" Nora asked.

"I don't even have a score!" snapped Mike.

He turned away from her, toward a stack of magazines on a table beside him. Movies, fashion, sports, fishing. Mike flipped through the whole stack, looking for something interesting. Even that was too loud, though. "Shhhhhhh," someone hissed. Mike slammed a magazine down, hard. He was getting mad.

Nora stood. "Can we take a walk?" she asked her mom. "Just around the corner?"

Before her mom could answer, Nora added, "We'll check in after ten minutes. We won't talk to strangers. Please? We need to get out of here." Somehow, she knew that Mike was about to explode.

He felt better as soon as he took a deep breath of the cool air outside. Sometimes all he needed was a change of scenery.

He followed Nora down the quiet street. Not much was going on out here. The dry cleaner on the corner was closed for the day. There was only one customer in the hair salon. After a little while, Nora stopped in front of a weird shop that Mike had never seen before.

The sign on the door looked like it had been there for a hundred years. It said

in handwritten letters. But there was a brand-new welcome mat out front. It said BELIEVE in bright red. Mike couldn't figure it out.

"Believe what?" Nora said. "That people ever go shopping here?"

Mike smiled for the first time in hours. "Let's check it out," he replied.

A bell rang when they walked into the store, but nobody came out to greet them. Nora followed Mike into a room full of what his mom would have called antiques, but his dad would have called junk. There were old mirrors, dented trunks, lamps without shades. Mike wrote his name in the dust on a table.

On a shelf near the back, there were a few cool things for sale. Whoopee cushions, disappearing ink, snakes in a can. Jokes and tricks. Instantly, Mike was in a better mood. Who knew there was a joke shop in town?

"Want a piece of gum?" he asked Nora, handing her a pack from the shelf. She reached for the stick that was poking out, and a hidden spring trapped her finger. Lots of girls would have screamed, but Nora cracked up. A gifted girl with a sense of humor? Mike had never met one of those before.

Mike shoved his hands in his pockets. He felt something crinkle. A five-dollar bill! "Look!" he said to Nora. "Let's see what we can get." He totally owed her for getting him out of that waiting room.

She picked up a set of plastic teeth with bright red lips. She wound them up and set them on the floor, where they hopped across the carpet, jaws moving up and down. Nora giggled. "Looks like they're talking!" she said. "Or chewing gum."

A man in a black shirt finally came to the counter. "Can I help you?" he asked. He had a gray beard and bushy hair sticking out like he'd had a shock. When he got closer, Mike could see tiny silver stars shining on his collar.

Mike remembered his manners. "We'll take the chattering teeth, please," he said, and felt in his pocket for the five-dollar bill. Suddenly there was another one. Ten bucks altogether! More money than he'd had since his last birthday.

Mike had no clue how ten bucks had appeared in his pocket, but he knew just what to do. "Make that two sets," he said.

The chattering teeth made the afternoon a little better. Mike and Nora raced their teeth on a windowsill while Mrs. Finn was in the dentist's chair. Mike still felt like a loser, but at least his teeth won first place.

When they got home, his parents had a serious talk with him. They talked about

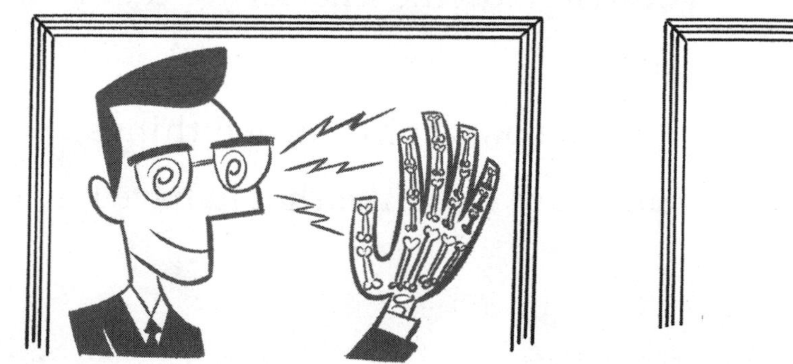

setting limits. They talked about getting him a tutor. It wasn't as bad as he'd expected. At least it wasn't anything new.

After dinner, Mike went outside to ride his bike in the driveway. Pretty soon Jackson came around the corner on *his* bike, twice the size of Mike's and painted with flames.

He bragged about the drills he'd done at soccer practice. He was faster and stronger than everyone else, if you believed what he said. He'd scored a thousand goals. He was ready for the Olympics. When he wasn't bullying, he was bragging.

Mike could hardly wait for him to leave.

After a while, he said, "Hey, did you know there was a joke shop downtown? Look what I got." He took the chattering teeth out of his pocket.

Somehow, they'd turned things around for him today. But Mike should have known their power couldn't last forever. He wound them up and put them on top of his picnic table, where Jackson could see them hop.

That's when they split into two and collapsed.

Chapter 3

SECRETS INSIDE

Jackson told everybody all about it the next day. "Watch out for Mike!" he warned other people on the lunch line at school. "Everything he touches falls apart."

He did a little demonstration of the way Mike's new toy broke the minute he touched it. "Can you trust him with a tray?" Jackson asked the cafeteria ladies. Some kids laughed, but Mike wanted to disappear. "I'm skipping recess," he told his friend Charlie. After lunch, he walked back to Mrs. Canfield's room.

"Everything okay?" she said.

"Just looking for some peace and quiet," Mike mumbled.

It was Nora's day to come to Mike's after school, and the rules were a little different at his house. The main thing was to stay out of his parents' way, because they were always on their computers. Once they did their homework, the kids could even watch a movie if they wanted to.

The thing was, Mike didn't want to. For once, he finished his homework sheets in one sitting. He really wanted to go back to The White Rabbit.

"To get more teeth?" Nora asked. "Really? You think another set will be any better?"

Mike just wanted to get something new. Something to shut Jackson up. A whoopee cushion would be good, he thought. "It'll be fun," he said, trying to convince Nora.

His mom had her doubts, too. "A joke shop that sells antiques?" she said. "I've never even heard of this place. But okay . . . I guess we can go . . ."

When they got there, Mrs. Weiss peered at the displays in the front window. There was a black top hat, faded by the sun, and a stuffed bunny that was looking pretty gray. "You're sure this is right?" she asked. "Looks like it's out of business."

"This is it," Mike said. The BELIEVE mat was just inside the door.

"I have an idea," said Mrs. Weiss. "See that coffee shop across the street? I'm going to take that empty window seat and wait for you there. I can keep an eye on you and also start grading some exams."

the White Rabbit
NOVELTIES ♣ SUPPLIES
WELCOME TO
the White Rabbit
OPEN
Believe

That was one good thing about spending afternoons with Nora, Mike thought. Kids like her got extra privileges. His mom would never have allowed this if he were alone.

The man with the wild hair was right at the front desk. Today, his shirt was midnight blue, with a row of half moons on the front pocket.

"Need more chattering teeth?" he asked, like he was reading Mike's mind.

"Yeah, they broke already," Mike said, surprised. "How did you know?"

"Lucky guess," said the man, holding out his hand. "Joe Zerlin. Good to see you again."

Mr. Zerlin began polishing a mirror, so Mike and Nora got a chance to wander around the store. Mike wondered where all these old things came from. Like the towering grandfather clock, still ticking away, or the big trunk with the padlock on it. The musty smell of the store reminded him of his grandma's house.

Or a museum, where a loud sound might shatter something valuable.

After a while, Mike went back to the shelf of joke stuff. He was looking at some plastic puke when Nora said, from a corner full of old books, "Did you hear that?"

She followed the sound around a corner and into a short hallway. "Come here!" she whispered. There was another room off the hallway, one they hadn't noticed before. It sounded like a pigeon was trapped in there.

Above its half-open door there was a banner that said:

Nora looked at Mike. "If there were really secrets, wouldn't the door be locked?"

It sounded like she wanted to go in. But kids like Nora never broke the rules.

What did Mike have to lose? He was always in trouble anyway.

"That banner . . . it's practically an invitation!" he said, pushing the door open. He and Nora walked in together.

What they found first wasn't a secret, exactly. It was more like a major surprise.

In the room there was a giant cage of white doves. They were cooing and pecking at their food.

It was pretty strange to find live animals in the back of an antiques store. But Mike didn't think about that at first. The room was crammed with so many other amazing things!

There was a huge trunk, overflowing with colored silks. There were stacks of cards, buckets of coins, bags of feathers. Boxes of every size, with tiny compartments hidden inside. A row of Magic 8 Balls, a section of stilts and wands, a pile of crazy wigs.

Mike walked from one end of the room to another, his eyes wide and his mouth hanging open.

A dusty tuxedo sat in the corner, a rubber hand dangling from its arm. A jar of eyeballs stared at Mike. He really hoped they weren't real.

There was a witch's broom hanging from the ceiling, and a cone-shaped hat, like a wizard would wear, sitting on a puppet's head. There was even a silver unicycle in the middle of everything. Part of Mike expected it to start zipping around without a rider. While he stood there dumbly, Nora answered the question he hadn't even asked yet.

"The trunks and mirrors," she said. "The doves. The hat and the rabbit. The name of the store, for Pete's sake. I can't believe we didn't see it before. It's got to be a magic shop!"

And Mike had thought a joke shop was cool!

He still remembered the time his friend Zack had a magician at his birthday party. Mike sat right next to him so he could watch what he was doing. No matter how carefully he watched, though, he couldn't figure out how the guy made things disappear. Or how he got flowers to bloom from the end of his wand.

Maybe this was Mike's chance to find out.

He and Nora found Mr. Zerlin near the front of the store. "Now we get it!" Mike said. "Everything here is for a magician's act, right?"

"I sell treasures . . . and tricks," said Mr. Zerlin mysteriously.

"Well . . . could you show us one?" Mike asked.

Mr. Zerlin's face lit up with a smile as bright as the chattering teeth. He took a box of cards out of his pocket. "Regular cards," he said, handing them to Mike. "Here, take a look."

They looked pretty normal to Mike. They felt normal when he shuffled them, too.

Mr. Zerlin took the deck and fanned out the cards, faceup, with a flourish. Suddenly he was more than a shopkeeper. He was a performer!

"They're in no particular order, right?" he asked. Mike and Nora both nodded.

Mr. Zerlin split the deck and placed the two halves side by side on a table. He took a card from one half and put it on top of the other. Then he pointed to the next card in the deck and instructed the kids, "Take a look at that one, but don't show me. Just remember what it is."

Nora took the card and guarded it as carefully as a paper in school. Only Mike could see: the three of spades.

"Now put it back, anywhere in the deck, and shuffle all the cards together," Mr. Zerlin told her.

Nora hid it in the middle of the deck. She shuffled the cards four times before she handed them back.

Mr. Zerlin fanned the cards out, just as he had before. “Let’s see if I can find it.”

He paused at the jack of diamonds. “Not this one . . .” he mused, rubbing his chin.

At the three of hearts he said, "Not this one, either . . ."

Then he moved ahead until he came to rest at the three of spades. Mr. Zerlin tapped it confidently. "This is the one," he said. "Am I right?"

"No way," said Nora, shocked. "I mean, yes —that's my card! But how did you do that?"

Mike imagined what it would be like to do something that nobody else knew how to do. He'd be a much cooler kid if he had a few tricks up his sleeve.

"Wish I could do that," Mike blurted out.

"Maybe you could and maybe you couldn't," Mr. Zerlin replied.

"What do you mean?" Nora asked. "Can't you teach us?"

"I can teach a magician," said Mr. Zerlin, as if that made things any clearer.

"But anyone can learn, right?" Nora pressed him. "It's not like we need magic powers or anything."

"Maybe you do and maybe you don't," said Mr. Zerlin.

Mike had wondered about that, too. Back at Zack's party, he had waited for the magician to slip and reveal his secrets. But his sleeves had been rolled up. There was nothing in his hands. He wasn't hiding anything, as far as Mike could tell. So how was he doing what he did? Mike never figured it out. He knew the magician couldn't really be magic . . . yet there was no other way to explain his tricks.

Mike was used to not understanding things. But he could tell it was bothering Nora.

"Well, how do you know if someone can do magic?" said Nora. "Is there some kind of a test or something?"

Mike rolled his eyes. If there was a test, he knew, Nora would get a perfect score.

"That's for me to know and you to find out," said Mr. Zerlin.

Even Mike was starting to wish that Mr. Zerlin would just give them a straight answer.

Then, for a moment, he dropped his mysterious manner. "Tell you what," said Mr. Zerlin. "I'll teach you a trick if you answer my riddle."

Chapter 4

THE RIDDLE

Mike loved riddles the way Nora loved Scrabble.

If he was supposed to remember something he'd learned last week, forget it. That's why his report card was always so bad. But a riddle was different. Everything you needed to know was right in front of you. You just had to look at it another way.

If the question was "What can you catch but never throw?" you needed to see the other meaning of "catch." The answer had nothing to do with a ball. The answer was "a fever." Mike loved how the answer to a riddle could be unexpected but totally obvious at the same time.

"I'm ready!" he told Mr. Zerlin.

"Bring it on," said Nora.

She probably did brainteasers every morning for breakfast. Mike hoped she didn't make him look slow.

"All right, then," the magician said. He took a stack of paper from under the counter and handed Mike and Nora each one sheet, along with a pair of scissors. "Can you cut a hole in this paper big enough to walk through?"

Uh-oh, thought Mike.

"That's not a riddle," Nora said.

"It's a challenge," said Mr. Zerlin. "And it's fine if you work together."

Anyone knew there was no way you could step through a hole in a piece of paper. Even with tiny margins all around, the hole would be no bigger than, say, both of Mike's hands spread wide. Maybe a baby could step through that hole, but nobody else.

Mike sighed. He looked at Nora blankly. He didn't really want this challenge. He just wanted to learn a magic trick before he left the store.

He cut the paper and ended up with a hole about the size of an index card. No good.

Nora was quiet. She wasn't having any luck, either.

Mr. Zerlin was watching Mike. "You can do it," he said.

Mike rolled his eyes again. Mr. Zerlin was a total stranger. He had no idea what Mike could do!

He glanced in the direction of the coffee shop, half wishing his mom would walk across the street.

He noticed the welcome mat again. The word BELIEVE glowed in the light from the shop window.

Mike let out a long breath. Fine, he thought. I can do it. I believe. Whatever.

Mr. Zerlin handed another piece of paper to Mike, folded in half the long way. He didn't say anything, just handed it over like he was giving an important clue.

Mike looked at the folded paper for a while. It was hopeless. Then, for some reason, he said, "Snowflakes!"

Nora looked at him like he'd lost his mind.

"Not the kind you see in winter," Mike explained. "The kind you learn to cut in kindergarten."

Mike folded the paper again and snipped. "What if I make a snowflake with a lot of empty space inside? Then what if all the ribs of the snowflake can be cut, and stretched out, sort of? Could that make a hole bigger than the original piece of paper?"

"I don't know," said Nora. "I don't really get it."

Suddenly Mike really *did* believe. This was the sort of test he could handle.

When Mike was doing riddles, he could tell when he was getting close to the answer. It was a sixth sense, like his mind was squinting to bring something into focus. Mike felt that way when he was cutting the paper.

It was totally unlike him, but he got absorbed in the work. No fidgeting, no fooling around. He tried every snowflake pattern he could think of.

Before he knew it, ten minutes had passed and Mike was surrounded by broken snowflakes. He liked that feeling of trying hard. But he wasn't any closer to figuring out the answer.

"Sorry," he said, putting down the scissors. He was giving up, the way he'd given up on a million things before.

So why was Mr. Zerlin looking at him like he'd done something right?

"I like the way you're thinking," said Mr. Zerlin, his dark eyes locked on Mike's. "Reaching hard for the answer that's right in front of you. I've never seen a kid come so close to solving that riddle."

Nobody said stuff like that to Mike. Ever.

"What about a zigzag?" suggested Mr. Zerlin.

Mike wasn't sure what he meant. But he could try one more time, he figured.

He folded another piece of paper lengthwise. He cut the edge in the shape of a lightning bolt, and opened it up hopefully. There was a hole there, all right, but not one you could step through. Unless you were twisted up, Mike thought. Doing yoga, maybe.

With another sheet, he cut in a straight line, almost at the top, from the fold to near the open edge. He stopped to think.

Then, below that, he made another cut in the opposite direction, stopping just before the fold.

He moved down the entire piece of paper, cutting until it was covered with what looked like stripes. Then he unfolded it carefully and cut down the middle, leaving only the very top and very bottom strips uncut.

With a deep breath, Mike separated the paper with his fingers. It opened and opened until it was the size of a Hula-Hoop. It really worked! He seriously couldn't believe he'd done it.

"I knew it!" said Mr. Zerlin joyfully.

Even Nora was impressed. "Awesome!" she said. "How did you do that?"

Mike stepped into the circle and bowed. "Magic, of course."

It really was a sort of magic, to be the one who pulled that off.

SHAPE SHIFT

BEGIN WITH A PIECE OF HEAVY PAPER, LIKE CONSTRUCTION PAPER OR CARDSTOCK. FOLD IT IN HALF THE LONG WAY.

STARTING ABOUT HALF AN INCH BELOW THE TOP EDGE, CUT IN A STRAIGHT LINE FROM THE FOLD TO THE OPEN EDGE OF THE PAPER, BEING CAREFUL NOT TO CUT ALL THE WAY TO THE OPEN EDGE.

NEXT, MAKE ANOTHER CUT, HALF AN INCH BELOW THE FIRST ONE, HEADING IN THE OPPOSITE DIRECTION. THIS TIME, YOU SHOULD CUT FROM THE OPEN EDGE TOWARD THE FOLD. AGAIN THOUGH, DON'T GO ALL THE WAY THERE.

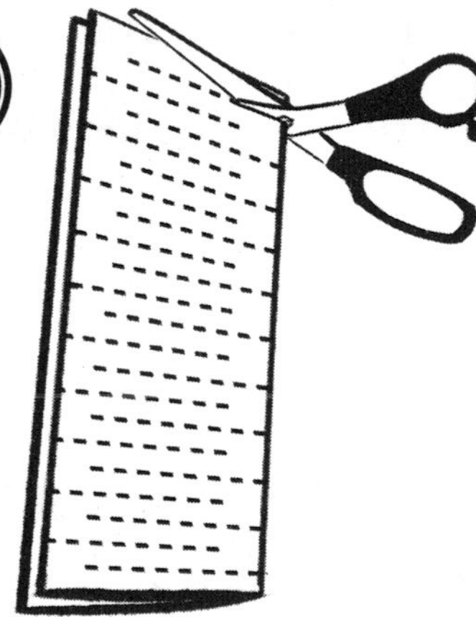

CONTINUE WITH THESE CUTS, BACK AND FORTH AND BACK AND FORTH, UNTIL YOU COME TO THE BOTTOM OF THE PAGE. YOUR LAST CUT SHOULD BE ABOUT HALF AN INCH FROM THE BOTTOM.

WHEN ALL THE CUTS ARE FINISHED, LAY THE PAPER ON A FLAT SURFACE AND SLOWLY OPEN THE PIECE OF PAPER. THEN, VERY CAREFULLY, SKIPPING THE VERY TOP AND BOTTOM STRIP, CUT ALONG THE LINE WHERE THE FOLD WAS. IT IS VERY IMPORTANT NOT TO CUT THROUGH THE TOP STRIP OR THE BOTTOM STRIP.

WHEN THE STRIPS OF PAPER BEGIN TO COME APART YOU WILL SEE THAT THEY UNFOLD IN THE SHAPE OF AN ENORMOUS CIRCLE.

HOLD THE CIRCLE OUT, TAKE A STEP THROUGH . . . *AND TAKE A BOW!*

"But it's all about the fancy cutting, right?" Nora said skeptically.

Mike didn't want to get into it right now. "So when do we learn the trick?" he asked Mr. Zerlin. He'd done what the magician had asked. How much longer would he have to wait? Mike wasn't famous for his patience.

It was awkward, though. Mr. Zerlin looked at Mike and Mike looked at Nora. She hadn't really solved the riddle. Would she get to learn the trick, too?

Nora brushed bits of paper off her hoodie. "Mike, I'm going to see if your mom will get me a snack," she said.

Mike watched her walk across the street, a bit confused. He had never won anything in his life, and now it felt like he'd won the lottery. He'd passed the test, and Nora hadn't?

Kids like Nora got special privileges, glimpses of the secret grown-up world.

But magicians had their own secret club, too. And after Nora left, Mr. Zerlin let Mike take his first peek in.

"Let's start with something basic. The Floating Cup Trick," said Mr. Zerlin.

Mr. Zerlin was a careful teacher, definitely better than Mike's last soccer coach. "That's it," he said. "No . . . more like this." He showed Mike, twisting his hand a bit. Within minutes, Mike was making a paper cup hover in mid-air!

Mr. Zerlin showed him how to practice in a mirror so he could see what his audience would see. He promised that Mike would get over the weirdness of talking to himself. "It's the best way for a magician to rehearse," he said.

He taught Mike to explain, for his audience, what he was about to do. "You tell them . . . but you don't tell them," Mr. Zerlin said. Somehow Mike knew just what he meant. A magician told a story, kind of. But not the whole story.

Mike kept glancing across the street. His mom and Nora were in the window of the coffee shop, with mugs of something hot. When his mom cleared the mugs off the table and put her papers in her bag, Mike knew it was time to go.

He still had some questions, though. Not about the trick—he pretty much had that down. He just kept thinking about that magician at the birthday party. Was there more to this than Mr. Zerlin had showed him?

He said thank you over and over again, until he finally asked what he most wanted to know. "So is magic really *real?*"

The magician's eyes crinkled when he smiled. "Maybe, maybe not."

Chapter 5

FLOATING ON AIR

Mike's dad called up the stairs after dinner, "Ten minutes till bedtime, Mike! What's happening up there?"

Mike was supposed to be reading, and keeping track of the minutes in a journal.

What was he really doing? "Just getting my act together for tomorrow, Dad!" he yelled. He knew how much his father dreamed of hearing those words. And it was true, in one way.

His dad probably imagined Mike lining up his pencils, or double-checking his spelling sheet. He wasn't thinking of the other meaning.

Mike was actually getting his *act* together. His magical act.

When he got home from The White Rabbit, Mike had raided the kitchen cupboard where his family kept the paper goods. Now he had a stack of Styrofoam cups in his room to practice with. Mr. Zerlin had used paper, but it was easier to punch holes in the Styrofoam.

Mike could already guess what Nora would say: Styrofoam wasn't good for the environment. So wasn't it better that he used them all up? That's what he would say if she brought it up.

Mike's door was closed. Even his window shades were down. Mike didn't want anyone to happen to see his trick when they were walking by his house. It had to be top-secret till he tried it at school.

Mike rehearsed one more time before he settled down with his book.

The first step was to poke a hole in the back of the cup with his thumb. Mr. Zerlin had explained that was the key to the trick.

Mike picked up the cup and faced the mirror on the back of his door. He felt a little silly talking to himself, but he had to practice to get it right.

"Watch me make this cup float in midair!" he announced to nobody. "Just an ordinary cup from my birthday party. See?"

Mike held the cup with both hands and displayed it for his pretend audience. He kept a straight face, like he wasn't hiding anything. Really, though, one of his thumbs was stuck in the hole he'd made. The other hand was covering it so no one could see.

"Two hands . . ." he said, ". . . and no hands!" He didn't have a good magic word figured out yet, but he could slip it in there at the big moment when he decided on one.

When he said "No hands!" Mike removed all his fingers from around the cup . . . except the thumb in the hole. He wiggled his fingers around the cup to show that they weren't holding on.

In the mirror, all he could see was a cup hovering eerily in midair, under a magic spell.

FLOATING on AIR

BEFORE YOU START THIS TRICK, YOU WILL NEED A LARGE PAPER OR FOAM CUP. WITH YOUR THUMB, POKE A HOLE IN THE CUP, ABOUT HALFWAY UP ITS SIDE. BE CAREFUL THE AUDIENCE DOESN'T SEE YOU DOING THIS.

NOW YOU CAN TELL YOUR AUDIENCE THAT YOU ARE GOING TO MAKE THIS CUP FLOAT IN MIDAIR. FIRST, MAKE SURE THAT NOBODY CAN WATCH YOU FROM BEHIND.

BEGIN BY PICKING UP THE CUP WITH BOTH HANDS. THE HOLE IN THE CUP SHOULD BE FACING YOU, WITH ONE OF YOUR THUMBS STUCK THROUGH IT. THE REST OF YOUR FINGERS ON BOTH HANDS SHOULD WRAP AROUND THE SIDE OF THE CUP TOWARDS THE FRONT.

HOLD THE CUP IN THE AIR APPROXIMATELY WAIST HIGH. THEN, SLOWLY BEGIN RAISING THE CUP WHILE LOOSENING THE GRIP OF THE NINE FINGERS THAT ARE NOT IN THE HOLE.

THE FINGERS OF BOTH HANDS SHOULD REMAIN CLOSE TO THE CUP AND MOVE IN A WIGGLING MOTION. THE HAND WITH THE THUMB THAT IS NOT IN THE HOLE CAN MOVE SLIGHTLY AWAY FROM THE CUP AND BACK AGAIN. TRY THIS IN A ZIG-ZAG PATTERN WHEN MOVING THE CUP UP AND BACK DOWN AGAIN.

WHEN YOU AND THE AUDIENCE ARE READY, YOU CAN "CATCH" THE CUP AGAIN WITH THE REST OF YOUR FINGERS.

DISPOSE OF THE CUP IMMEDIATELY AFTER THE PERFORMANCE SO THE HOLE IN THE CUP IS NOT EXPOSED.

He could see the trick—the thumb in th hole. But if he did it right, his audience woul only see magic.

"Abracadabra!" he tried saying in the mir ror the next time he did the trick. "Alakazam. That made him laugh, every time he said it He sounded like some guy in a fairy tale! Bu he had his first trick down, he was pretty sure

Tomorrow, he would test it at lunchtime.

While the rest of his class had social stud ies, Mike met with Mr. Malone, a math teache who tutored students one-on-one. Maybe h could help Mike. That was supposed to b good news. But now everybody in his clas would know—if they didn't already—that h needed extra help. That he was having extr trouble.

Could magicians make themselves invis ble? Maybe Mr. Zerlin could teach him tha trick next.

Mike answered all of Mr. Malone's questions. "Yes, I can add and subtract. Still working on the times tables." While they were talking, Mike was playing with a rubber band. He stretched it and snapped it till the rubber band was loose and flexible. He hoped the teacher wouldn't notice. But then it shot across the room.

He was really tired today, Mike said. That was why he couldn't stop fidgeting. But that wasn't really why he was about to jump out of his skin. He couldn't wait—he *could not wait* —to work magic during fourth-grade lunch.

Best-case scenario? He did the trick right and people thought it was cool. Worst-case scenario? He did it wrong and no one ever let him live it down. It was a risk. But it wasn't like Mike had some great reputation to protect.

He always met Charlie and Zack at the same fourth-grade cafeteria table. Charlie tossed his lunchbox on the table and got right down to business. "What do you have?" he asked Mike. They weren't supposed to trade, but Charlie had a tried-and-true technique for trading under the table.

"Ham sandwich," Mike said. "Grapes. Cheesy popcorn."

"Oh yeah! Popcorn for a . . . fruit snack?"

No deal. Mike changed the subject before Charlie could talk him out of his lemonade. "Wait till you see what I've got! I learned a magic trick yesterday and I want to show you guys."

Zack was finally out of the hot-lunch line. "A magic trick?" he said. "Not like those chattering teeth, right?"

"Nope. Much better. In a minute, though." Mike knew that when his friends dug into lunch, they wouldn't notice he was preparing his cup under the table. If Charlie could trade lunches under there, he knew there was enough cover to get the cup ready. Mike's back was to the wall, so nobody could see him from behind.

"We still need some kids for our soccer team," Zack said with a mouth full of grilled cheese. "There are just enough of us now, but if anyone gets sick we're in trouble. First game is coming up. Guess who's on the other team?"

"Ugh," said Mike. He knew who, instantly. "Jackson?"

"Yup. He's gonna kill us if we don't have enough kids for substitutions. By the end of the game, we'll be falling all over the field. No way every kid should play every minute of a game."

Charlie went in for the big question. "Any chance you'll change your mind, Mike?"

"My parents could take you to practice," Zack said. He let that sink in. Then he added a little something extra, in a low voice so no one else would hear. "You wouldn't have to go to Nora's."

Yesterday, Mike would have done anything to get out of spending afternoons with Nora. Now he wasn't so sure. His parents thought he couldn't handle school and soccer at the same time. If somehow he convinced them to let him play, would he ever get to do anything else? Like magic?

"I don't think so . . ." Mike said.

Zack looked at the table. "We'll keep looking, I guess."

Mike took a bite of his sandwich and quickly stuck his thumb into the hole in the cup. "So, you guys want to see something cool?" he said.

"The magic? Yes!" Charlie said.

Mike put on a magician's voice. "Observe as this Styrofoam cup floats toward the ceiling!"

It was more dramatic than what he'd practiced in his room, but it just came out that way. Suddenly, Mike felt like a different person.

He began by wrapping his fingers around the cup. Then, as he'd practiced, he let them go. "Hocus. . . pocus!" he said.

Charlie and Zack stared at the cup. "It's floating!" Charlie said, like he couldn't believe his eyes.

Mike moved it up. He moved it down and around. It looked like the cup was following his hands.

"How's it doing that?" asked Zack.

A kid from the next table turned around to look. "Check it out!" she said, nudging her friend. Mike didn't even know who those kids were. Now they knew who he was, though.

Mike had an idea. "Clap your hands and it'll come down," he told one of the girls. At her clap, he guided the cup down toward his sandwich.

"Awesome," said a boy from Mike's class.

"Do it again!" someone else called from across the aisle.

"Show us how to do it!" Charlie and Zack chimed in.

Mike shook his head wisely, in his best impression of Mr. Zerlin, but it actually hurt his face not to smile. He felt like he could smile for the rest of the day.

"I can't," he said. "It's magic."

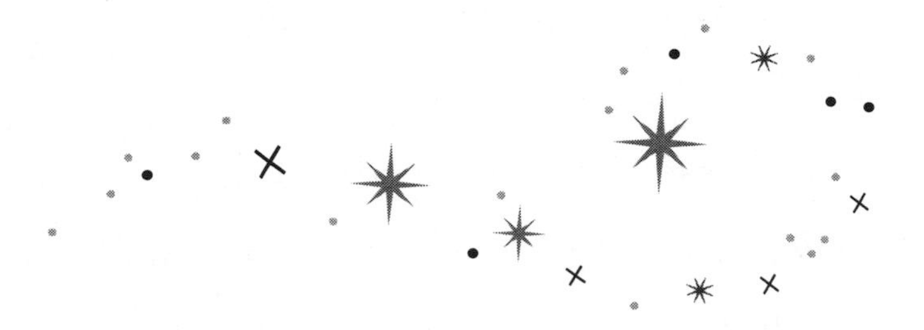

Chapter 6

READY FOR MORE

Only one person was unimpressed.

Mike was throwing out his garbage, just before the bell rang, when a ball of tinfoil bounced off his head and into the trash.

"Nice trick," Jackson said. "Didn't fool me, though. I know just what you did."

Was he even watching? Mike wondered. And how would Jackson know anything about magic?

"Oh really? Just wait till next time," Mike said, bluffing.

"Next time?" Jackson laughed. "There's more?"

"You won't believe what I can do," said Mike.

"Can't wait to see this," said Jackson. "I'll need a front-row seat." Shaking his head, he went to join the rest of his class.

Next time, Mike thought. He liked the sound of that.

All afternoon, kids were high-fiving Mike in the hallway. He didn't care that he struck out playing kickball during gym. He didn't care that Mrs. Canfield gave him a warning for leaving his reading minutes at home.

The only thing that could get him down was Jackson. He was hanging around the back door after school. When he saw Mike meet up with Nora, he beamed. No way they'd get away from him now.

"You walking home with your girlfriend?" Jackson asked Mike.

He zoomed past them on his flame-covered bike, then circled back around. "Falling under her magic spell?"

Luckily, Mike and Nora lived close to school. They didn't have to put up with him for long. But Jackson's eyes lit up when he saw them walk up to the same house. Mike had a feeling Jackson wouldn't let him forget it for a long time.

"Have fun at your playdate," he mocked. Jackson made some gross kissing sounds as he pedaled off toward his own house, right around the corner.

Talk about awkward. "Sorry . . ." Mike said as Nora unlocked the door.

"For what?" asked Nora. "He's just a bully."

"He's been after me all day," Mike said. Actually, Jackson had been after him for a lifetime. But Nora didn't need to know that.

"Probably saw your magic trick at lunch," said Nora. "He can't stand to see anyone do anything he can't do."

Nora had only known Jackson for a few weeks. So how did she get that already? Maybe she was even smarter than Mike thought.

Nora opened the fridge, looking for snacks. "You did a great job, by the way," she added. "I loved the trick. But can I give you one piece of advice?"

That was the last thing Mike wanted. But what could he say? "Okay . . ."

"You need a better magic word."

"I know!" he said, laughing. He'd have to ask Mr. Zerlin about that. "Hey, Nora," said Mike, as she handed him a yogurt. "I'm sorry about the trick."

"What?" she asked.

"The way I got to learn it, but you left the store?"

Nora shrugged. "That riddle made no sense to me at all! So I didn't think he would teach me anything. It's totally fine. I don't think magic is my thing." She let it go, just like that. It took Mike's breath away. Magic wasn't her thing? Well, maybe it was his.

Then Nora's mom came downstairs. "How about we go to the library?" she said, mostly to Nora. Turned out Nora had a giant bag of books to return. More books than Mike had read in the past two years.

The library had never been his favorite place, not since he got too old for stories with pictures. Kids his age were always reading books that were two inches thick, but Mike couldn't deal with those. By the time he got to the middle, he couldn't remember what had happened at the beginning. What he liked most were comic books, but that section of the library was pretty small.

Nora sat at a computer with a list of titles. She looked them all up, one by one, while Mike started his homework. When he saw his parents, they would check that it was finished.

"Has your class started doing book reports yet?" Nora asked him.

Mike had a bad feeling about that. Those reading minutes . . . what was he supposed to be reading, anyway? Was it a book for a project? He really couldn't remember.

"I don't think so," Mike said.

She looked at him curiously. "All the fourth-grade classes are doing them. What kind of books do you like to read?"

"I don't know . . ." Mike said. "Books with a lot of action, I guess."

"What about books on magic?" Nora suggested. She was full of good ideas. "I can find them for you," Nora added helpfully.

Turned out there was a whole *section* on magic! Mike found a book of magic tricks and a biography of Harry Houdini, master magician and escape artist. With books like these, even Mike could manage a book report.

Reluctantly, he returned to his homework. As soon as he'd written out the final spelling word, he started to think about the next trick he'd do at school. A coin trick or a card trick? He couldn't decide. Was he ready for a grand escape? The books could tell him all he needed to know.

READ
RETURN

But the librarian at the counter handed his card back when he tried to check out. "The system says you have a lost book. Until you pay for it, I'm afraid you can't take anything else."

That book—full of sports facts—wasn't lost at all. Mike was pretty sure it was under his bed. But he wouldn't be able to get it back in time to check out the magic books today.

"I'll put them on hold for you," the librarian said kindly. "You can come and get them tomorrow. Or whenever you're ready."

Mike was quiet on the trip home. He was really disappointed. He took out his spelling words and pretended to look them over, so he wouldn't have to talk to Nora. What kind of kid couldn't manage to return a library book? he wondered.

He cheered up when his dad got home. Proudly, he showed off his finished spelling sheet. And now he could try his trick again!

"I have something to show you," Mike told his dad, leading him to the living room couch. "You stay here."

Mike stood on the other side of the coffee table and made another Styrofoam cup float up. He could do it with a little less preparation now, and he added some stage talk, too. "Hold on now—don't fly away," he said to the cup. "Don't leave me!" He made it look like the cup was headed for the ceiling.

"Impressive," said Mr. Weiss.

Mike told him, "I did it in the cafeteria today at school. People really believed I was . . . powerful."

"Where'd you learn how to do that?" his dad asked.

"From the magician who owns The White Rabbit," said Mike.

"The antiques store?" said his dad.

"Well, sort of. But there's a different room, hidden in the back, where you can get stuff to do magic tricks."

Suddenly he thought of something. The library had closed by now. But there were probably books at The White Rabbit, too.

"Dad, do you think you could take me there? I think it's open pretty late. There's something I want to get."

His dad checked the time. "I just got home, Mike. I have to cook tonight. I have a big day tomorrow . . ."

He hadn't said no.

"It will be really quick," Mike promised. "I can pay for it myself." Sometimes that convinced his dad, and Mike had some emergency funds in an old pair of sneakers. "You can even wait in the car if you want."

His dad sighed. "All your work is done?"

There was that confusion about the book report. Mike didn't know when it was due. He didn't even know if he was supposed to be doing it.

"All taken care of," he assured his father. He'd figure it out later.

Mike's dad took his keys from his jacket pocket. "Let's go before Mom gets home."

The car pulled up outside The White Rabbit just as it was starting to get dark. The street lights flipped on, and Mike could see Mr. Zerlin inside, turning lights off. He looked like he was in a hurry.

Mike knocked on the door, which was already locked. He waved wildly until Mr. Zerlin spotted him.

"Are you closing?" Mike called through the glass. "I just wanted to get something, really fast."

"Ready for more?" asked Mr. Zerlin. Again,

Mike had that weird feeling that the magician knew what he was thinking.

"Yes!" he called. "I did the trick at school and it was perfect!"

"I must hurry," said Mr. Zerlin. He stepped outside the door and closed it behind him. He wasn't letting Mike in after all. "But I thought you might like this."

He pressed something into Mike's hands and scurried down the street, calling over his shoulder, "Now you see me, now you don't."

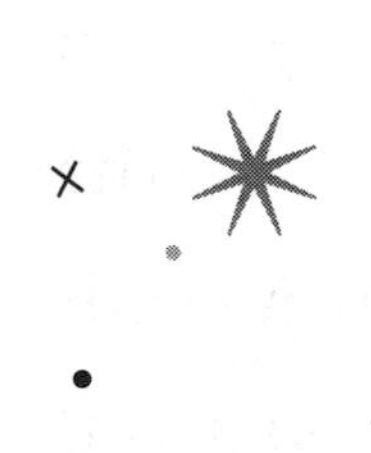

Chapter 7

THE VANISHING COIN TRICK

It was a book.

Somehow, Mr. Zerlin had known that Mike wanted a book.

Mike didn't know how Mr. Zerlin knew or where he had gone. But this book—*The Book of Secrets*—was much better than anything he'd seen in the library. It had silver lettering on the cover, like tinfoil, and yellowed pages

the
BOOK
of
SECRETS

that made it look like many magicians had read the book before Mike.

There were more tricks inside than Mike had ever dreamed of. He could do a different trick in the cafeteria every day if he wanted.

He thought about homework for about two seconds. How would Nora know the whole fourth grade was doing a project? he wondered. It wasn't like the teachers would tell her, would they? She didn't know what she was talking about.

With that worry off his mind, Mike turned on his desk light and opened the *Book of Secrets*. It began with a quote from someone named Goethe. "Magic is believing in yourself. If you can do that, you can make anything happen." Mike smiled. He had a good feeling about this. Turning the page, he found the Vanishing Coin Trick. So that answered his first question: coins or cards? Cards could wait for the next time.

Down in the kitchen, his dad was clattering around. His mom came home and unloaded the dishwasher. Mike could hear his parents talking about their days, then the silence of them both checking their messages. But he didn't really take any of it in. He was too busy learning how to make a coin disappear.

The trick called for double-sided tape, which Mike just happened to have in his desk. He put both of his hands faceup and, with a tiny piece of tape, stuck a quarter right in the middle of his middle finger.

In the mirror, Mike showed both hands. It looked like he was holding the coin—the tape was all rolled up so no one could see it was actually stuck.

Then he clasped his hands together to make it look like he was dropping the coin from one hand into the other. He even closed the left hand to make it seem like he'd caught it.

Really, though, he still had the coin stuck to the middle finger of his right hand. He put that hand in his pocket and scraped the coin off quickly. His left hand was still clenched, as if he was holding something.

"With this magic dust, I'll make that coin disappear!" Mike told his pretend audience. The right hand came out of his pocket now, and sprinkled imaginary magic dust over the left. Time to try out another magic word. "Shazam!" Mike said as he opened his left hand dramatically.

There was nothing there, of course—the coin was still safe in his pocket. He spread open his fingers and moved them around to make it clear he wasn't hiding anything.

This was the point where people would start to applaud, Mike thought. Tomorrow, he

could be a star again. But he had to make sure the trick was perfect. And Jackson would be watching, so he couldn't slip up.

Mike lined up some action figures in front of the mirror so he could practice making eye contact. He tried to make it look natural when he was holding the coin at the start of the trick. Would people notice when he was scraping off the coin in his pocket? Maybe it would be better to talk during that part, he thought. Then people would concentrate on what he was saying, not what he was doing.

Suddenly, his mom's voice came up the stairs. "Are you okay, Mike?" she asked. "I've already called you twice. It's dinnertime!"

Mike quickly unstuck the coin from his hand and opened his door. "Just working hard," he said. "Lost track of time." She didn't need to know what he was working on. Not yet.

the VANISHING COIN

BEFORE YOU BEGIN—*AND WITHOUT YOUR AUDIENCE SEEING*—YOU WILL NEED TO ATTACH A SMALL PIECE OF DOUBLE-SIDED TAPE TO THE BOTTOM OF A COIN. WITH YOUR PALM UP, STICK THE COIN TO YOUR MIDDLE FINGER, ABOUT HALFWAY UP.

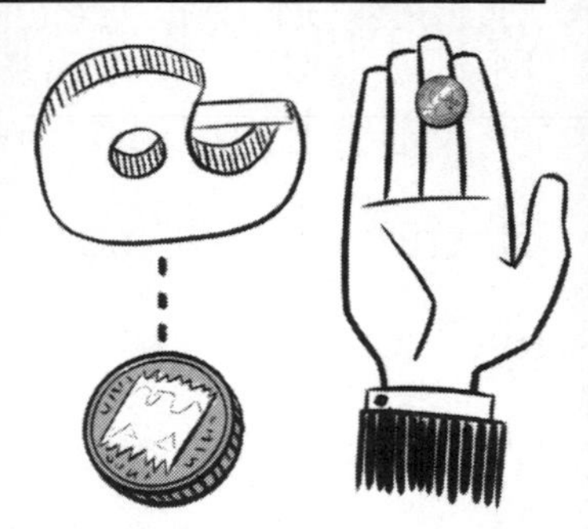

THE FIRST STEP IS TO HOLD OUT BOTH OF YOUR HANDS, PALMS UP AND FINGERS TOGETHER, TO SHOW THE COIN TO THE AUDIENCE.

NEXT, PLACE THE HAND WITH THE COIN PALM DOWN IN A FLIPPING MOTION OVER THE PALM OF THE OTHER HAND. IT WILL LOOK LIKE YOU ARE MOVING THE COIN FROM ONE HAND TO THE OTHER. MAKE THE RECEIVING HAND LOOK AS IF IT IS CATCHING AND HOLDING THE COIN. REALLY, THOUGH, THE COIN WILL BE IN THE SAME PLACE IT HAS BEEN ALL ALONG.

NOW REACH INTO YOUR POCKET WITH THE HAND THAT STILL HOLDS THE COIN. TELL THE AUDIENCE THAT YOU ARE LOOKING FOR MAGIC DUST IN YOUR POCKET. WHILE YOU'RE DOING THIS, SCRAPE THE COIN AND TAPE OFF YOUR FINGER AND LET IT DROP INTO YOUR POCKET.

REMOVE THE HAND WITH A HANDFUL OF INVISIBLE MAGIC DUST, AND SPRINKLE THAT DUST OVER THE HAND THAT'S STILL CLOSED.

Remember! THE AUDIENCE BELIEVES THAT THIS OTHER HAND CAUGHT THE COIN A MINUTE AGO. BUT WHEN YOU SPRINKLE THE MAGIC DUST OVER THIS HAND, AND OPEN UP THE FINGERS . . . IT'S NOT THERE! OPEN YOUR OTHER HAND TO SHOW THAT THE COIN ISN'T THERE, EITHER. LEAVE YOUR AUDIENCE ASTOUNDED.

Note: YOU CAN USE REGULAR ADHESIVE TAPE BY FOLDING A SMALL PIECE WITH THE STICKY SIDE OUT.

◆ ◆ ◆

The next morning, Mike found a bunch of coins and slipped them into the front pocket of his backpack, along with several tiny knots of double-sided tape. Couldn't hurt to have some extras, he thought. In case something went wrong.

And, actually, *everything* went wrong. Before he even attempted the trick.

First, Mrs. Canfield collected homework from her class. "Notes for your book projects," she told the kids. "I'll look them over to make sure you're off to a good start."

Mike watched as kids handed in stacks of index cards held together with rubber bands. Mrs. Canfield met his eye. "Yours too, Mike," she said.

"I left them at home," he lied. "Can I bring them in tomorrow?"

Mrs. Canfield sighed. "First thing in the morning," she said.

Mike wasn't sure how he was going to pull this off. Could he do a report on *The Book of Secrets*? He was too embarrassed to ask. And too distracted by thinking about his trick.

Mr. Malone, the math guy, arrived just before lunch. Turned out Mike had to take a test during his lunch period, instead of going downstairs with everybody else. "Just to see where you are right now," Mr. Malone said. "So we know where to start our work together."

Where am I? Mike thought bitterly. I'm right here. Hungry for my sandwich. And hungry, he had to admit, for some of that feeling he'd had yesterday.

By the time recess rolled around, Mike was mad. Maybe that's why he climbed over the playground fence to get the paper airplane he'd thrown over. Maybe that's why he

NCIPAL

ignored the teacher on duty, calling him back. Maybe that's why he ended up in Ms. Scott's office again. The second time in three days. There would be no recess for him tomorrow.

Nora came over after school. By some miracle, neither of them had homework. But it took them awhile to find something to do. Finally, she wandered into his garage and came out with a soccer ball. "Want to play?" she asked.

Mike set up his goal and tried to shoot against her, but she was quick. Is there anything she can't do? he wondered.

As he missed another shot, Jackson came by on his bike. His eyes lit up when he saw them. Yesterday they'd been at Nora's, today they were at Mike's. Mike could tell Jackson had figured it out: He spent every afternoon with Nora Finn.

"Too bad you can't play soccer with the boys this year," Jackson laughed. "But at least you can play with the girls. They're more your speed, anyway."

"Oh yeah?" said Mike indignantly. "Bet you can't score against Nora."

Jackson grinned. "What's it worth to you? A quarter?" He flung his bike down on Mike's lawn.

Jackson dribbled the ball around the yard. On his first shot, Nora caught the ball. He whistled. "Not bad," Jackson said.

He moved the ball back toward the street, and took his time with it. He kicked it in the air and headed it, just to show off. And then, when Mike had started to think he wouldn't bother shooting again, he got the ball past Nora's outstretched hands.

"Score!" yelled Jackson triumphantly, pumping his fist in the air. "Time to pay up, big guy," he said to Mike.

Mike's backpack was on his front stairs. He had to have a quarter in there with all his coins. He found one pretty quickly. But he also found his scraps of tape . . . which gave him an idea. He knew how to make up for his rough day.

He walked back to Jackson and gave him the quarter. "Here you go," Mike told him. "Fair and square."

Jackson took it and headed for his bike. "Should have bet at least a buck," he muttered.

"Hey, can I show you something?" Mike said. "Can I see that quarter for a second?" In his hand, he'd hidden a piece of tape.

Jackson frowned. "I guess . . ." Slowly, he gave it back to Mike.

Mike stretched his hands out and showed Jackson his quarter, which was now invisibly taped to his finger. "Here's your quarter, right?" he asked.

"Obviously," said Jackson.

Mike clasped his hands, as he'd practiced in the mirror, to make it look like he'd moved the coin. But it was really still in the same hand, which he put in his pocket.

"It's right here," Mike assured Jackson. He looked at his left hand, which was now in a fist. "But let's see what happens when I sprinkle a little magic dust over it, okay?" He pretended to get the magic dust out of his pocket with his right hand. Then he sprinkled the dust over his fist. He decided on a magic word Jackson was sure to know. "Abracadabra!"

When he opened his fist, the coin was gone.

Chapter 8

SHARING SECRETS

"Hey, give it back!" Jackson said.

"I can't," said Mike. "It disappeared." He pretended to look for it on the ground. Even in his pocket.

"You stole my money!" Jackson insisted. "Give it back!"

"It's gone. Vanished into thin air," Mike said. He was loving this.

Jackson's face was turning red. "You did some trick and you took what's mine!" he snapped.

Mike shrugged. "I'm really sorry," he said.

"Yeah, you sound really sorry."

"It's just a quarter," Nora piped up.

Jackson whirled around. "You stay out of this!"

"There's nothing he can do," Nora pointed out. "It's gone."

Jackson grabbed his bike off the grass. Mike and Nora could hear his tires squealing like a race car as he rounded the corner toward his house.

Mike and Nora high-fived.

"Did you see his face?" Nora laughed. "He was furious!"

Mike had known Jackson forever. Even when they were little, Jackson was the one who pushed other kids around. Or took their toys. Getting him back, for once, was sweet.

"He'll keep nagging me about that quarter until he gets it back," Mike said.

"You think he'll bother?" Nora asked.

"You don't know him like I do," Mike told her. "He has to have his own way."

"Maybe you can trick him again?" Nora suggested.

Mike paused. He hadn't thought of that. There were plenty of tricks in *The Book of Secrets*. It would drive Jackson crazy to keep getting fooled.

Mike hadn't decided if he would show the book to anyone. But Nora would understand it better than anyone else he knew. She'd met Mr. Zerlin herself. And he could really use her help, picking out a good trick.

"Can I show you something?" he said.

"Sure," said Nora, following him inside.

They tiptoed past Mike's mom's office—she was in there on the phone—and went upstairs to Mike's room. He took *The Book of Secrets* out of his sock drawer and handed it to Nora.

"Whoa . . ." she said, running her hands over the silver letters on the cover. "Where did you get this?" She could see it was something special.

"Yesterday, after we left the library, I begged my dad to take me back to The White Rabbit," Mike explained. "I thought I might be able to get a magic book there even after the library was closed. Mr. Zerlin was leaving. But he had this book there, just waiting for me. He gave it to me and disappeared down the street."

Nora was quiet for a moment. "That's really weird," she said. "How did he know? It's like he knows magic, but he *is* magic. He knows secrets and he *has* secrets."

Mike knew exactly what she meant.

"There are tons of tricks in there," Mike said. "Some of them have to be right for Jackson!"

Nora opened the book and glanced at the first page. Then she closed it quickly, like she knew she shouldn't read any further. "And the whole book is *full* of them?"

Mike didn't know much about magic, but he knew magicians didn't tell their secrets. They took a special oath or something,

he was pretty sure. They promised not to share their tricks.

But a magician also needed a person he could trust. A person who was in on the trick. One of Mike's friends could do that. Charlie or Zack. But which one? Not both. Could he really trust either of them more than Nora? Even grown-ups trusted Nora.

"You can read the book," he said after a minute. "It's okay. But you have to promise not to tell. Ever. Magicians are careful about their secrets."

She put her hand up like she was taking a vow. "I swear," she said seriously. "I will never share these secrets."

Now they were new neighbors, sort-of friends, and sworn partners in magic. Mike just hoped that Jackson Jacobs would never figure that out.

"So . . . you want to see how I made the coin disappear?" Mike asked.

She watched intently as he did the trick. Mike taped the quarter to his finger. He made the fist, dropped the coin in his pocket, and sprinkled the magic dust.

Nora shook her head. "I never would have figured that out," she said. "How did you learn that?"

"The way you learn anything, I guess," said Mike. "I read the book and followed the directions. And I practiced, too." He didn't mention the action figures.

"But I thought . . ." Her sentence trailed off, and Mike knew *just* what she thought.

"I'm just not good in school, okay?" he said, annoyed. "I can't sit still. So sometimes I miss things. But I can learn. I'm not stupid, if that's what you were thinking."

Nora blushed. "That's not what I thought," she said. "I saw you do that riddle. Maybe you just . . . understand things that other people don't understand. I'm a little like that, too."

Mike wanted to stop talking about this. "I hear you're pretty smart," he said lightly. "So that makes two of us. And you're great at soccer, too!"

Nora sighed. "I was on a team at my old school," she said. "But by the time I moved here, it was too late to sign up."

"You should come with me tomorrow," Mike said. "I told Charlie and Zack I'd go to their first game, even though I'm not playing. Zack's dad is the coach—he'll know how to get you on a team."

Nora smiled. "Thanks, Mike," she said. "So how about that magic trick?"

Nora sat at his desk, while Mike sprawled on the floor with *The Book of Secrets*. "I don't even know where to start," he said, flipping through the pages. "Let's see. We could make a coin sweat," he said. "That would really freak Jackson out. Or how about this . . . we could make it feel like a ghost was tapping him on the shoulder!"

"I don't think he'd fall for that," said Nora. "Can I see?"

Mike passed the book up to her. "What about this one?" she said. "Wait, how do you even do that?" she wondered. "Hide the spectator's card under a Band-Aid on your arm? Cool!"

Mike looked over her shoulder. "There's a section here called Mind Magic . . ."

"No! I don't want to read Jackson's mind!" Nora said. "You really want to know what he's thinking?"

"I guess not. Hmm. Wait a minute. I've got it!" said Mike. He turned the page and stayed at the desk so he and Nora could look at a trick together. Silently, they both read through the instructions. Then they grinned at each other. It was perfect.

But before they could try it, they heard Mike's mom coming up the stairs. She walked swiftly down the hallway and stood outside Mike's door with her hands on her hips.

"That was Mrs. Canfield on the phone," she told Mike. "What's this about a book report?"

Chapter 9

TAKING NOTES

"Mrs. Canfield needs at least ten notecards by the end of the day tomorrow," Mike's mom said. "Or she'll take ten points off your grade."

She sighed and crossed her arms. "This wasn't the plan, Mike. I thought you were trying to get off to a good start this year."

Mike had that hopeless feeling that he'd had outside the principal's office. No matter how hard he tried, he could never do anything right. He wished Nora would go home before he had a full-on fight with his mom. But Nora totally saved him.

"I know what the assignment is," she assured Mike's mom. "I think I can help." It was like she was working some magic of her own. Before Mike knew it, his mom was walking back down the stairs, completely trusting that the notecards would be done. Mike was as shocked as he'd been when he walked into the back room at The White Rabbit.

He wanted to do his report on *The Book of Secrets*, but Nora stared at him when he suggested it. "No, that won't work," she said. "The school library opens early. You need to get something there."

Mike didn't like her bossy tone, but they were partners now.

Mike's dad drove them to school the next morning. It was so early that the parking lot was empty and a custodian was polishing the floors. Mike's dad dropped them off, and within ten minutes Nora found Mike a short book about Houdini.

She showed Mike how to take notes on the index cards, too. One idea per card, Nora explained. "Pretty simple," she said. "When you're all done with these notes, you'll type them into a computer and write the report." That's what her class was doing, anyway.

Mike had a hard time keeping focused on the cards, though. Houdini was awesome! Nobody could figure out how he did any of his famous tricks. And he did some pretty amazing stunts, too. Like locking himself up in a trunk and having people throw it off a bridge! Somehow, he always managed to get away.

By the time the bell rang, Mike had actually read a big part of the book. Now he just had to go back and finish the notes before

Harry Houdini
Born: March 24, 1874
Budapest, Hungary
Died: October 31, 1926
Detroit, Michigan

the end of the day. He didn't want to lose ten points. Or the privilege of going to his friends' soccer game.

Mike already knew he'd be spending recess in the principal's office. He sat in his usual chair, in front of Mrs. Warren. "You're working hard," she said approvingly as he spread notecards all over the place. She slipped him a lollipop, too.

Before he went back to Mrs. Canfield's room, Mike stopped in the hallway for a drink of water. He could feel somebody watching him while his face was in the fountain. Jackson, of course. "So when am I getting my money back?" he asked with a sneer.

"You'll see," said Mike. He was trying to sound mysterious, not mocking. But Jackson took it the wrong way.

"Is that right? Well, you'll see this!" He ripped the notecards out of Mike's hands.

"Looks like some homework to me," he said. "Late again, big guy? Hey, maybe magic will help you get these back."

Jackson crumpled them up and stuffed them in his jeans pocket. Then he got swept up in a group of second graders on their way outside.

Mike almost crumpled, too. There was no way Mrs. Canfield would believe what happened. And he didn't even want to know what his parents would say. So what was he supposed to do?

During silent reading time, he opened the Houdini book and rewrote as many notecards as he could remember. Then he did a couple more, to get to ten. He had to get to that game! He and Nora had a plan for getting back at Jackson. And now it was more important than ever.

When Mrs. Canfield met his eye, Mike looked away. But she didn't say anything. He wasn't supposed to be taking notes during silent reading. Maybe she really meant it when she said she was on Mike's side.

Mike finally handed in the notecards, just before the bell, and Mrs. Canfield smiled. "I knew you could do it," she said. "Tomorrow you can get started on your report."

Did magicians grant wishes? Mike wondered. He really wished that the report would write itself. And that Jackson would get what he deserved, someday.

Their arrangements after school were complicated. Mike walked to Nora's house, and Nora's mom took them to the soccer game. She had to leave them there alone, though, because it was her night to work late. Coach Larsen, Zack's dad, would keep an eye on Mike and Nora during the game. Then, when it was all over, Mike's dad would take them home. Mike even had his library book—the one with the sports facts—to slip into the library slot on their way back.

Mike found Coach Larsen standing on the sidelines with a clipboard. "This is my next-door neighbor, Nora," Mike told the coach. "She's new in town. And she loves soccer, but she missed the deadline for signing up."

"I happen to know that one of the girls' teams is down a player," Coach Larsen told Nora. "A goalie. Maybe you could take her place? I'll need to look into it."

Nora beamed. "That's my favorite position," she said. "Let me know what you find out!"

Coach Larsen tapped the brim of Mike's baseball cap. "We miss you, buddy! It's just not the same without you." Mike was glad to be missed. For a minute he even wished he was playing.

Then he remembered *The Book of Secrets* and his excitement at learning all its mysteries. "Maybe next year," he told the coach.

Whether they won or lost, Coach Larsen's team always had a good time. He made his team run backwards and do jumping jacks before the game.

On the other side of the field, Jackson's team, in blue jerseys, was huddled together.

Jackson broke away from his team and paced along the edge of the field. "He hates to lose," Mike whispered to Nora. "Looks like his whole team is pretty intense."

Jackson glared at Mike and Nora when he spotted them in the bleachers. Then he came up to them during a water break. "Got my quarter, man?" he said. "I could use some money for the snack shack."

Mike turned his pockets inside out. "I'm broke," he said.

"What'd you spend my money on? Some new notecards?" His laugh was more like a cackle.

His coach called him back. "Jackson!" he said sharply. "You're going in!"

Things didn't go well for Jackson in the game. Charlie stole the ball from him and scored. Jackson shot three times, but he kept missing the goal.

At the next break, he found Mike and started in on him again. "If you don't give my money back, you know what? I'm calling the police."

Like the police would care about a missing quarter! Jackson was losing his cool.

Now it was time to move in on him with some magic. Mike hoped he and Nora could pull it off even though they'd barely practiced.

"Fine," he said, like it was killing him. "I'll give it back."

"About time," said Jackson.

Mike's pockets were empty, as Jackson had just seen. "Do you have a quarter, Nora?" he asked.

She was expecting the question.

Nora handed him a five-dollar bill. "Sorry—I don't have anything smaller," she said.

Jackson's eyes grew wide. Was that all for him?

Mike held up the five to show Jackson. But before Jackson could reach for it, Mike folded it in half from left to right. Then he folded it in half again.

"What's this? Origami?" Jackson said.

Mike did one more fold, this time from top to bottom, toward himself.

Then, slowly, he shook a quarter out of the five-dollar bill. "Ta-da!" said Mike. "This is yours, right? I made a little change."

UNITED STATES OF AMERICA
QUARTER DOLLAR

Jackson's eyes were wide. "Where did that come from?" he said. "How did you do that? That was five bucks . . ."

Mike handed it to him. "Take it. It's yours."

Jackson took a step back. "That's not my quarter."

Just as he had conjured a quarter, Mike had suddenly conjured a braver self.

"Take it or leave it, Jackson," Mike said firmly.

He pressed the coin into Jackson's hand.

"You got what you asked for," Mike pointed out. "Twenty-five cents. That's what we bet on."

"But not like *that* . . ." Jackson sputtered.

Just then his coach blew his whistle. Jackson was back in the game.

Nora called after him, "Don't spend it all in one place!"

MAKING CHANGE

BEFORE YOU BEGIN, HIDE A COIN BEHIND THE BOTTOM RIGHT CORNER OF A DOLLAR BILL. *(OR, IF YOU PREFER, A LARGER BILL).* YOUR THUMB WILL HOLD THE COIN, WHILE YOUR OTHER FOUR FINGERS WILL BE IN FRONT OF THE DOLLAR BILL. YOU MAY HOLD THE BILL THE SAME WAY ON THE OTHER SIDE WITH YOUR LEFT HAND.

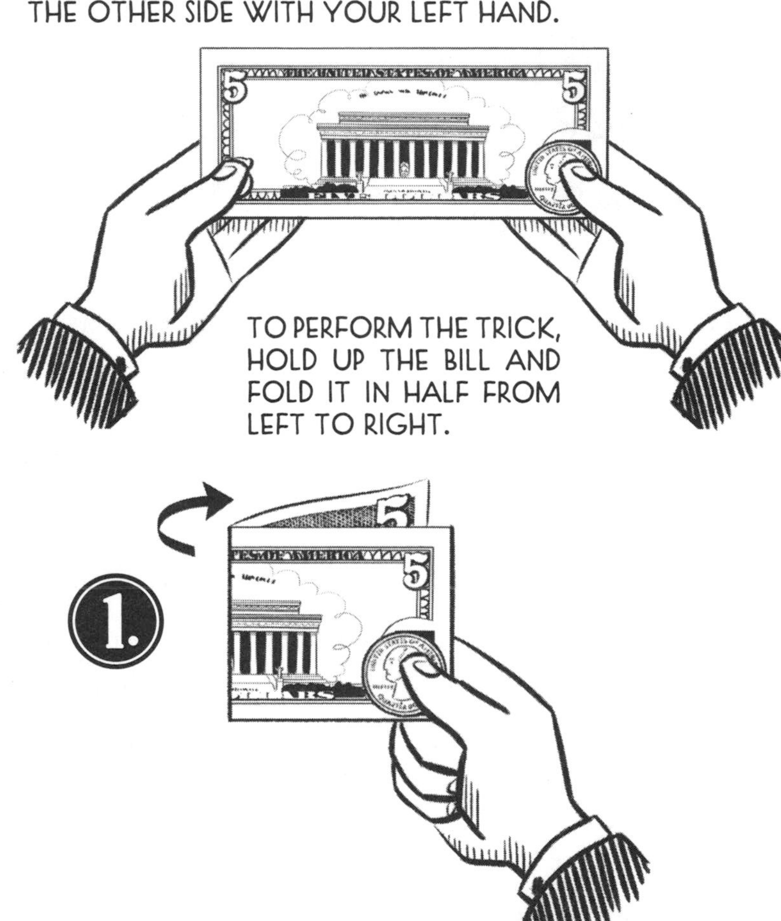

TO PERFORM THE TRICK, HOLD UP THE BILL AND FOLD IT IN HALF FROM LEFT TO RIGHT.

THEN FOLD IT AGAIN, MAKING SURE TO KEEP THE COIN HIDDEN THE WHOLE TIME.

FINALLY, FOLD THE BILL A THIRD TIME, THIS TIME TOWARD YOURSELF, FROM TOP TO BOTTOM. NOW THE COIN WILL BE IN THE MIDDLE OF AND COVERED BY THE FOLDED BILL.

HOLD YOUR LEFT HAND PALM UP, AND DROP THE COIN FROM THE BILL INTO THAT OPEN HAND.

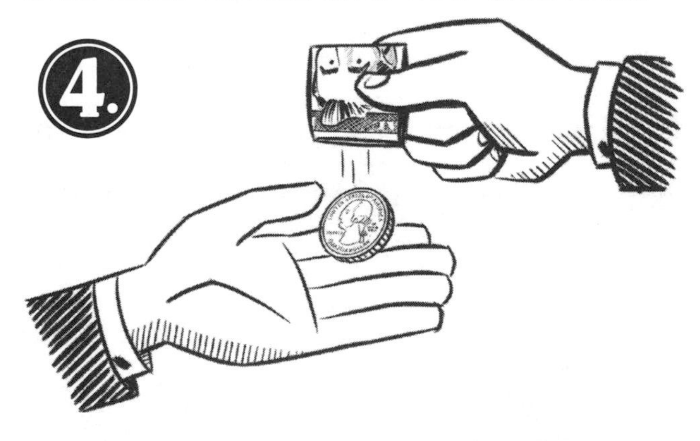

Note: *THE BILL USED FOR THIS TRICK SHOULD BE PRE-FOLDED AHEAD OF TIME AND THEN UNFOLDED AGAIN.*

Chapter 10

THE PHONE BOOTH

Mike felt a little giddy for the rest of the game. It was like the time he'd had a caffeinated soda by mistake, and it kept him up all night. His heart was racing, and his mind was racing, too. He couldn't believe what they'd just done.

Normally Mike was a nice kid. He didn't like to make people feel bad. But making Jackson feel bad . . . that was what Mike called justice.

Maybe Jackson wouldn't bother him again for a while. He could walk to school, or play in his yard, without getting teased. He could be friends with a girl without Jackson insisting she was Mike's girlfriend. Jackson had his money now. But Mike had put him in his place for once.

Nora seemed happy, too, but she was focused on something else. "'Ta-da' just doesn't seem magical," she said. "That's what you say when you hand someone a piece of paper. I think you need a word that sounds special. Like you're summoning magic when you say it. 'Presto,' maybe? Would that be better?"

Mike stood up to cheer on Charlie, who'd just scored another goal.

He'd already tried a bunch of magic words, but none of them felt right. He told Nora about the time he saw the magician at Zack's party. "He asked Rachel Joyce to say 'Abracadabra,'

Mike remembered. "But she stumbled over the word. The magician acted all confused. He said, 'Have a banana?'" I could say that . . ."

"That doesn't sound like a magician," said Nora, frowning. "More like a clown. I think I'll make a list of possibilities. Put all the options on the table. And then you can decide."

There was another whistle, and suddenly the teams were walking toward the middle of the field, shaking hands. They weren't supposed to act happy if they'd won, but Mike knew how Charlie and Zack must be feeling. A big win in their first game. A big win against Jackson! If the soccer league didn't have strict rules, they would have been celebrating big-time.

"Great game!" said Mike as his friends came up to the bleachers. "Way to go!"

Charlie took a long drink from his water bottle. "We survived without you!"

Mike was dying to tell them about tricking Jackson, but he'd have to do it another time. Everyone was rushing to get home now. That was one of the problems about playing soccer. The games were on school nights, and they ended pretty late. It drove all the parents crazy.

Coach Larsen came up to them with a bag full of soccer balls. "Need a ride home?" he asked Mike and Nora.

"No, thanks," said Mike. "My dad will be here any minute."

Most of the kids were piling into cars and vans, taking off their muddy cleats before closing the doors. On the edge of the parking lot, Jackson unlocked his bike. Nobody offered him a ride, even though they were going back to the same neighborhood. It would be a long way home on a bike.

There was only one way out of the parking lot, and a line of cars formed at the exit. Mike peered into each one, looking for his dad. There was no sign of him yet, but Mike did spot someone who looked like Mr. Zerlin, with his hair sticking up. Mike wondered what the magician was like when he wasn't at The White Rabbit. Did he have kids of his own?

"Where's your dad?" asked Nora. "Is he always late?"

"No!" said Mike. "I'm sure he'll be here soon."

"This is why I need a cell phone!" Nora said.

"You don't have one, either?" Mike asked. That was something they had in common. His parents didn't trust him with one yet. They didn't want to be tracking it down at the lost and found, they said.

"My parents are pretty low-tech," said Nora. "They say I have to wait till junior high, at least."

Mike wondered if his dad had forgotten about them. What will we do if he has? Mike thought. Practices were held at school, but soccer games were on this field, way out at the edge of town. They really wouldn't be able to walk home.

There were only a few cars left now, and Nora was getting worried. "Do you think there's anybody on the field?" she asked. "Groundskeepers, maybe? Adults who can help us?"

It was hard to see, since it was getting dark, but Mike didn't notice anyone else around. And then he did. It was the shadowy figure of Jackson, circling back on his bike.

Jackson didn't really get in fights. But . . . he could. It wasn't hard to imagine. It made Mike a little nervous for them to be all alone out here with only Jackson for company. He was mad about the magic. He was mad about losing the game. He was mad about looking like a fool. It could be a dangerous combination. Mike really wished his dad would show up now.

There was a full moon rising, and in its light Mike noticed something he hadn't seen before. Way out on the opposite edge of the field, almost hidden in the trees, there was a box. A small building. A shed?

Nora followed his gaze and said, "What's that?"

"I think it might be a phone booth," Mike said. Not that he knew how to use one. All he knew about phone booths was that they were where superheroes changed into their capes. Still . . . there should be a phone in a phone booth, Mike thought. Right? That way they could find his dad.

He followed Nora across the grass and watched as she opened the glass door, hinged in the middle. "Yeah . . . there's a phone in here!" she reported. "But I think you have to pay to use it."

Pay phones, Mike thought. He'd heard his parents talk about them. "How much does it cost?" Mike asked.

"A quarter," said Nora. She came out of the phone booth and closed the door. This was a problem. They didn't have a quarter. They only had a five-dollar bill. Mike took it out of his pocket to look at it. Useless. He jammed it back in.

Jackson was riding toward the exit now. "Should we run after him?" Nora asked.

"I don't know," Mike said miserably. He couldn't imagine what Jackson would say if they asked for—begged for!—the quarter at this point. Someone could get hurt.

"He's our only hope," Nora pointed out. "Do you have any other ideas?"

"My dad wouldn't forget me!" Mike said.

"Sometimes in movies, people find spare change in pay phones," Nora remembered.

"There's a slot that returns your extra money, I think. If you put in too much to start with. We should try it, just in case."

She stepped back inside the phone booth just as a cloud covered the moon. Man, it was dark out here. Mike put his hands in his pockets, suddenly cold. They seemed different from before, somehow. What was in here? There was a jingling sound, like he was carrying some rocks.

Or coins. Suddenly there were coins.

Mike rummaged in his pockets, and came out with quarters. Quarters that hadn't been there a second ago.

Nora came out of the phone booth to find Mike staring at his open hands. "What happened?" said Nora. "Where did they come from?"

"I don't know!" Mike exclaimed. "I had five dollars, and now I have . . . these."

So how did they get there?

Mike could only think of one thing. Magic.

Not the kind he was starting to learn, but the other kind.

The kind that maybe Mr. Zerlin knew.

Mr. Zerlin, who might have been that guy in the car.

But how could he know? thought Mike. How could he do this?

It didn't make sense, but there was no other way to explain it.

Mike felt the way he'd felt the first time he saw a magician do a trick. It couldn't be true . . . but it had to be true.

He was all about riddles and hidden meanings, but he also knew that sometimes they weren't there.

Sometimes you had to take things for what they were.

Sometimes you had to stop asking questions and call your dad before things got too freaky.

Mike stepped into the phone booth just as his dad's car came into the empty lot.

Just as another cloud passed over the brilliant moon.

And just as he noticed the letters shining on the glass.

Believe.

The End

Thank you for reading this
FEIWEL AND FRIENDS book.
The Friends who made

possible are:

Jean Feiwel, *Publisher*
Liz Szabla, *Editor in Chief*
Rich Deas, *Senior Creative Director*
Holly West, *Associate Editor*
Dave Barrett, *Executive Managing Editor*
Nicole Liebowitz Moulaison, *Production Manager*
Lauren A. Burniac, *Editor*
Anna Roberto, *Assistant Editor*

FOLLOW US ON FACEBOOK OR VISIT US ONLINE AT MACKIDS.COM.

Mike's next magic trick—convincing his parents he's responsible enough to ride his bike to The White Rabbit alone—will take something truly incredible!

Don't miss the second book in the Magic Shop series!

Is it possible that Mike could be related to Harry Houdini—the greatest magician ever? But when he's dared to prove it, Mike's in the type of bind that only magic can help him escape!

Don't miss the third book in the Magic Shop series!

Mike's magic skills are about to face their biggest challenge yet—the school talent show!

Coming soon!
Don't miss the fourth book in the *Magic Shop* series!